Junaid in Lahore

Ailsa and Alan Scarsbrook

A & C Black · London

My name is Junaid Dah, and I'm eight years old. I live in Lahore in northern Pakistan. It's a very big, busy city, and more than four million people live here.

There are six of us in my family. My dad works in the High Court and has an office in Lahore. Here he is, outside our flat. He's about to go to work so Mum and my little brother Furqan have come outside to say goodbye. Furqan is only three but he's already a real little chatterbox.

I've got two sisters. Seemal is the eldest, she's fourteen and quite grown-up. Zillah is seven, she's my favourite sister and I like playing with her – most of the time, anyway.

to Islamabad

River Ravi

USSR

CHINA

AFGHANISTAN

PAKISTAN

Islamabad

Lahore

Pakpattan

Multan

Sui

INDIA

IRAN

Karachi

ARABIAN SEA

Pakistan Minar

Badshahi
Mosque

Fort

OLD

Anarkali
Bazaar

Punjab High Court

my school

Seemal's school

zoo

to airport

grandma's
house

bazaars

canal

parks

0   1 kilometre

N

our flat

SAMANABAD

to Pakpattan and Multan

We live in a flat in Samanabad, which is one of the modern suburbs of Lahore. Our flat is on the ground floor of a small block, with only one other flat above it.

Big brown and white doors lead into the yard where Dad keeps the car, and where we can play with our friends. From the yard you walk onto the verandah. Our flat has a living room, two bedrooms, a kitchen and a shower room. I have to share a bedroom with Zillah and Furqan – I don't mind sharing, but I don't think Zillah likes it much.

We haven't got a garden, but luckily there's a park just across the road from the flat. There are lots of parks and squares in Samanabad, where we can ride our bikes and play games.

My dad is always the first one up in the mornings – he gets up before sunrise every day to say his prayers. He wears a shirt, and baggy trousers called shalwar, and puts his prayer topi on his head. Then he takes off his sandals and kneels on a prayer mat.

My family are Muslim and we pray to Allah. We face Mecca when we pray. Mecca is a city in Saudi Arabia, it's a holy place for Muslims. When Dad's finished praying, he reads the Koran, the Muslim holy book, before breakfast.

In termtime Mum wakes us up at 6 o'clock in the morning, and we get dressed in our school uniform. I wear a blue shirt and short grey trousers. Zillah wears a blue and white dress, but when she's ten she'll wear kamiz (tunic), shalwar, and dupatta (a scarf) like Seemal.

I'm always in a rush to eat my cornflakes – I have to be ready when the Suzuki van arrives to take Zillah and me to school. I pack my school books into one bag, and some food for break in the other. Today Mum's given me some egg sandwiches and an apple, with fruit juice to drink.

At 6.40 the van arrives, with some of our friends already inside. Mum and Dad pay the driver to take us to school and collect us later.

The ride to school takes about ten minutes. When I get there, I dump my bags in the classroom and go out into the playground to look for my friends. My best friends are Gulfraz, Raza and Sohail, and we usually have time for a game before the bell goes at seven o'clock for assembly. We all line up in our separate classes and say some prayers, then it's time for lessons.

There are more than 2700 children in my school,
the youngest are five and the oldest are sixteen.
There are 66 children in my class – I share a desk
with Raza. Here we are having a science lesson. I
like science, but maths is my favourite subject. We
also have lessons in Urdu, English, art, social
studies, music and Islam which is religious
education.

My school is a private one; Mum and Dad decided
to send Zillah and me here because they wanted us
to learn English as soon as we started school. In the
state schools you don't learn English until you're
ten. Mum and Dad have to pay fees to send us
here, and they have to buy all my text books and
exercise books as well as pens and pencils.

I like games lessons – I'm learning to play cricket and football. We also play lots of different team games and circle games. One of my favourites is when you have to run really fast round the circle and get back to your place before you get caught by the person chasing you.

In summer, school starts at seven o'clock and finishes at one. In winter it lasts from eight until two. Because we start so early, we have a break in the middle of the morning. We have our milk and sandwiches, and go out into the playground. Then there are more lessons, and when school is finished, the Suzuki van takes us home.

In summer, Zillah and I get home soon after one o'clock. Sometimes Mum sends me down to the shop in the market to get some chapattis. I like that because it's always fun to watch the dough being rolled out and slapped onto the wall of the tandoor to cook. The tandoor is a special round oven – this one's kept heated by a gas flame in the bottom. When the chapattis are cooked, the man gets them out with metal rods.

Then Zillah and I get changed out of our school clothes and have something to eat. Sometimes Mum gives us meat and vegetables with chapattis, or sometimes we have kebabs. After that we have some fruit and a cold drink from the fridge. When the weather's hot, we usually all lie down on charpoys and have a sleep.

At about five o'clock, when it has cooled down a bit, I like going to the park to play. Last week I bought a kite with my pocket money. I wanted to show Raza, Sohail and Gulfraz how high it could fly, and I surprised them all – it flew higher and higher until it looked really tiny. We could still see it quite clearly, though, because the sun was shining through it.

Every evening my sisters and I have to read a bit of the Koran. We have to learn to read it in Arabic. Most children go to the mosque to read the Koran, but Dad has asked the Imam to give us private lessons at our house. The Imam is a very learned man – he knows a lot about the Koran.

When we read, I wear my topi and my sisters cover their heads with their dupattas. Furqan can't read yet, but he still likes to come and sit with us.

I have to do homework after school. Last night I had to do a project on leaves so I collected them from lots of different trees and stuck them in my book. It gets dark at seven o'clock, but I managed to get quite a lot of leaves before then. I was still sticking them in at ten.

During the day, my mum is busy at home looking after Furqan and keeping the flat tidy. She usually does the washing after breakfast when we've gone to school.

Later in the morning the vegetable man brings his barrow down the street. He sells bhindi, cabbages, aubergines, small pumpkins called kidoo, and lots of other vegetables depending on the time of year.

Today Mum needs to buy some tomatoes. Furqan is going outside with her because he loves watching the man weigh out vegetables. The man holds the scales in one hand whilst he puts the tomatoes on with the other.

Mum is giving us chicken biryani for our evening meal. She makes it by cutting the chicken up into small pieces, then cooking them with onions, rice and spices.

Mum sits down to work on a little stool called a pirhi. When she makes her own chapattis, she sits on the pirhi and rolls out the dough on a round board. Then she cooks them on a hot plate called a tawa. At the moment she's using the tawa to cook vegetables.

We all sit round the table in the living room to have our evening meal. Mum's made a tomato salad and chapattis and a bowl of yogurt to go with the biryani. She's cooked chips too – my favourite food. My mum learned how to make chips when she visited England last year. For pudding there's zirda, which is sweet yellow rice with almonds and sultanas, then we all have a cup of tea or fruit juice.

After the meal Seemal and her friend Aneela have a giggle looking at the family photograph album. They say that there are some really funny photos of Dad when he was young.

We watch TV most evenings. Zillah and I like to
watch the cartoons and programmes about
animals. We watch English and American films,
too, but our favourite is the wrestling. I usually
watch until bedtime.

On Thursdays we can stay up late because there's
no school next day. Friday is the Muslim holy day.
Just before we go to bed, Dad tells us a story about
saints and heroes who lived a long time ago,
and how they were always kind and helpful and brave.

My dad works at the law courts in the centre of Lahore. He is a special kind of lawyer called a barrister. His job is to defend people who are on trial accused of crimes like stealing or cheating or murder.

Dad has worked at the Punjab High court for fifteen years. In court he wears a black gown over a black suit. He makes notes on each case, and has to check them before the judge arrives and the trial begins. A trial can last from a few hours to a week or more.

Dad usually finishes work between three and four o'clock. In the evening he often does some of the shopping. He likes to buy some fresh fruit every day. At this stall he's getting bananas, apples, and some juicy kainus, which are a special sort of orange. If Dad's in a good mood he sometimes gets some sweets for us. There are lots of small shops near home, and Dad knows quite a lot of the shopkeepers and their families.

On the days when he's not in court, Dad has an office in Lahore where people can come and talk to him. He also works in the courts at Pakpattan and Multan. Pakpattan is 200 km from Lahore, and Multan is 350 km away, so Dad has a lot of travelling to do.

Dad works in a modern court at Pakpattan.
Several cases are tried there every week. The men
wearing black berets are police officers, and the one
on the right is guarding the men on trial. My dad is
defending these men – they are accused of robbing
a bank.

Dad's clerks stand near him, holding his papers.
The clerks help Dad by working as his secretaries
and carrying messages for him.

When Dad is working at the Pakpattan courts, he
lives in our second house which is in Pakpattan. We
all go there in the school holidays. A lot of our
friends have two homes, like we do.

The house at Pakpattan is big, with two storeys. Dad has an office at the top, with his own special staircase leading up to it. That means his clients don't have to go through the house.

In the middle of the house there's an open yard. It's great for games when our friends come round. This game is called kokla-chaupakee. Zillah and the others squat in a circle, leaving a space for me, and everybody faces the middle.

I have to run round the outside holding a twisted piece of cloth which I drop quietly behind one of the others. He's not allowed to look round, but just has to feel for it. If he finds it, he picks it up and chases me, trying to hit me with it until I get back to my place.

Friday is our special day for prayer, and my dad takes Zillah and me to the mosque. Dad wears his loose shirt and shalwar. We always go to the same mosque when we're in Pakpattan – it's quite famous.

Before we go into the mosque we have to perform wuzu, which is a special kind of washing, to purify ourselves. We cover our heads and take off our sandals. Then we go inside and try to find a space because the mosque is packed with people.

Dad doesn't usually work on a Friday – after we've been to the mosque he likes to take the whole family out for the rest of the day. In termtime, when we're in Lahore, we sometimes go and play cricket in the park. We have to use a big ball because Furqan's only three and he can't manage a little ball yet. After we've finished the game, we get ice-creams from the little shop in the park.

Lahore is called the City of Gardens because there are so many parks. Sometimes Dad takes us to Iqbal park where there's a big tower called the Pakistan Minar. There is a lift to the top, but I'd rather race Zillah up all 300 stairs. At the top you can see right over Lahore, and look down at all the tiny people below. The Minar looks smashing at night when it's all lit up.

Sometimes we go to the Anarkali bazaar. It's the most famous bazaar in the city, and Mum and Seemal love wandering round the shops and stalls. There are always all kinds of exciting things for sale – embroidered jackets, glass bangles, and jewellery made of gold and silver. Seemal likes looking at all the lovely colours of the saris and kamiz and shalwar.

Last month for a treat, Mum and Dad took us to the zoo. My favourite animal was the elephant, and Furqan wanted to take the baby zebra home. We couldn't do that – but we watched it eat its dinner. The keeper had just put some hay in the feeding trough.

It's quite a big zoo, and we had to do a lot of walking to see all the other animals. By the end we were hot and thirsty, so we went to the Zoo Cafe to sit down. Mum and Dad had 7-Up, but Zillah and Furqan and I had lovely mango juice. Then as the sun went down, we set off for home and our evening meal.